If You See a Kitten

John Butler

PEACHTREE
ATLANTA

For Joanna

Ω

Published by
PEACHTREE PUBLISHERS
1700 Chattahoochee Avenue
Atlanta, Georgia 30318-2112
www.peachtree-online.com

Text and illustrations © 2002 by John Butler
First published in Great Britain in 2002 by the Penguin Group
First United States hardcover edition published in 2003
First US trade paperback edition published in 2015

Illustrations created in acrylics

Printed in October 2014 in China at South China Printing Co Ltd.

10 9 8 7 6 5 4 3 2 1 (hardcover)
10 9 8 7 6 5 4 3 2 1 (trade paperback)

Library of Congress Cataloging-in-Publication Data

Butler, John.
  If you see a kitten / written and illustrated by John Butler.
        p. cm.
  Summary: Illustrations and brief text present appropriate responses to
     a variety of animals, from pudgy pigs to slithery snakes.
  ISBN 978-1-56145-108-1 (hardback)
  ISBN 978-1-56145-838-7 (trade paperback)
        [1. Animals—Fiction.]   I. Title.
        PZ7.B97718If 2003
        [E]—dc21   2002011552

If you see a
cuddly kitten...

say,

"*Ahhh!*"

If you see
a pudgy pig…

say,
"Peee-
ew!"

If you
see a dozing
dormouse...

say,

"Shhh!"

If you see some
slimy slugs...

say,

"*Yuck!*"

If you see
a pretty
peacock...

say,

"*Oooh!*"

If you see
a slithery
snake...

say,

"*Yikes!*"

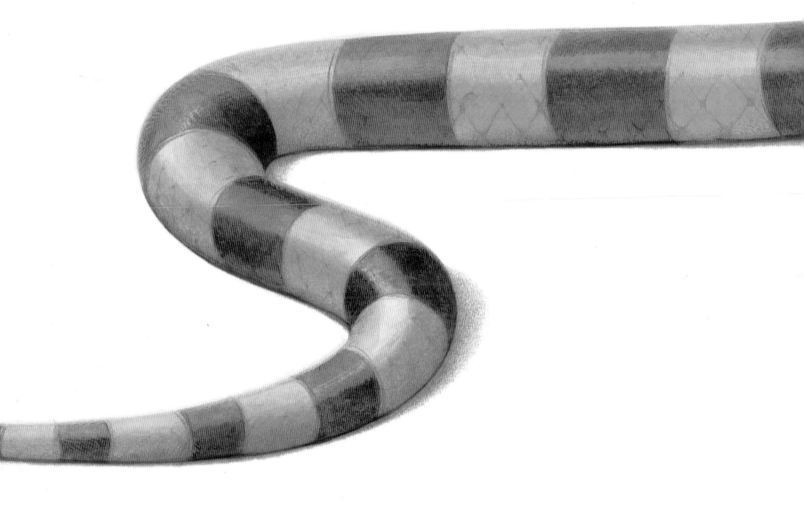

If you see a
          prickly porcupine...

say,

"*Ouch!*"

If you see
an enormous
elephant...

say,
"*Wow!*"

If you see a
spooky spider...

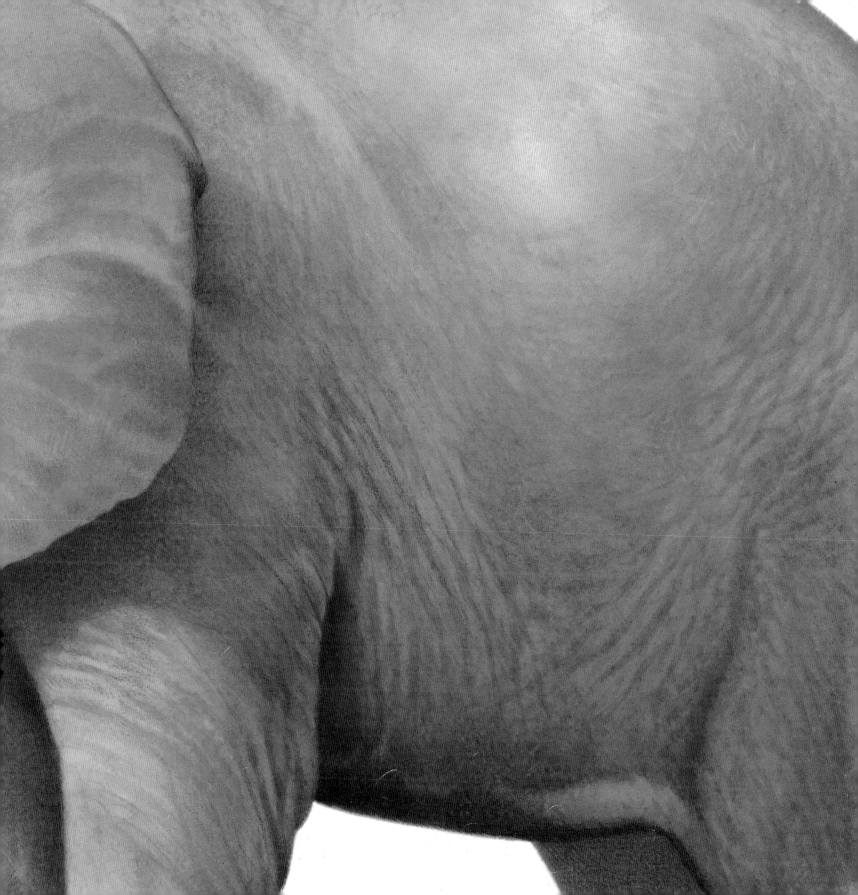

say,
"Eeek!"

And if you see
a crabby
crocodile...

say,
"HELP!"